# TEENAGE MUTANT NINJA TURTLES

## MICHELANGELO

Story by **Brian Lynch**
Artwork by **Andy Kuhn**
Colors by **Bill Crabtree**
Lettering by **Shawn Lee**

 Spotlight

**ABDOPUBLISHING.COM**

Reinforced library bound edition published in 2015 by Spotlight,
a division of ABDO, PO Box 398166, Minneapolis, Minnesota 55439.
Spotlight produces high-quality reinforced library bound editions for
schools and libraries. Published by agreement with IDW.

Printed in the United States of America, North Mankato, Minnesota.
112014
012015

THIS BOOK CONTAINS
RECYCLED MATERIALS

**IDW**

## LIBRARY OF CONGRESS CATALOGING-IN-PUBLICATION DATA

Lynch, Brian (Brian Michael), 1973-
    Michelangelo / writer, Brian Lynch ; artist, Andy Kuhn. -- Reinforced library
bound edition.
        pages cm. --  (Teenage Mutant Ninja Turtles)
    Summary: "Michelangelo explores New York City and finds even more
mysteries"-- Provided by publisher.
    ISBN 978-1-61479-340-3
1.  Graphic novels.  I. Kuhn, Andy, illustrator. II. Teenage Mutant Ninja Turtles
(Television program : 2012- ) III. Title.
    PZ7.7.L95Mi 2015
    741.5'973--dc23

                            2014038218

**Spotlight**

A Division of ABDO
abdopublishing.com

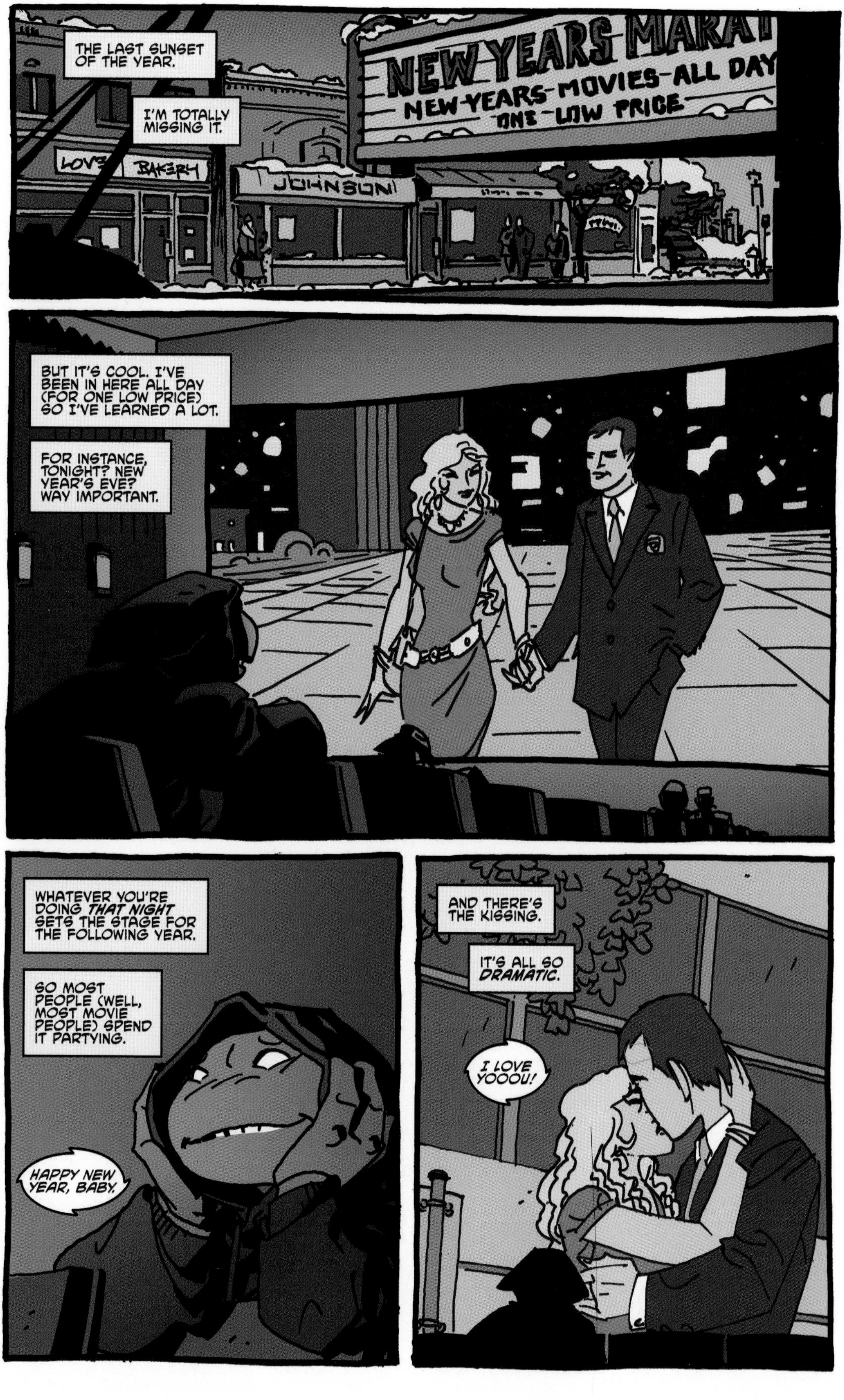

THE LAST SUNSET OF THE YEAR.
I'M TOTALLY MISSING IT.
NEW YEARS MARAT
NEW YEARS MOVIES ALL DAY
ONE LOW PRICE
BAKERY
JOHNSON
BUT IT'S COOL. I'VE BEEN IN HERE ALL DAY (FOR ONE LOW PRICE) SO I'VE LEARNED A LOT.
FOR INSTANCE, TONIGHT? NEW YEAR'S EVE? WAY IMPORTANT.
WHATEVER YOU'RE DOING *THAT NIGHT* SETS THE STAGE FOR THE FOLLOWING YEAR.
SO MOST PEOPLE (WELL, MOST MOVIE PEOPLE) SPEND IT PARTYING.
*HAPPY NEW YEAR, BABY.*
AND THERE'S THE KISSING.
IT'S ALL SO *DRAMATIC*.
*I LOVE YOOOU!*

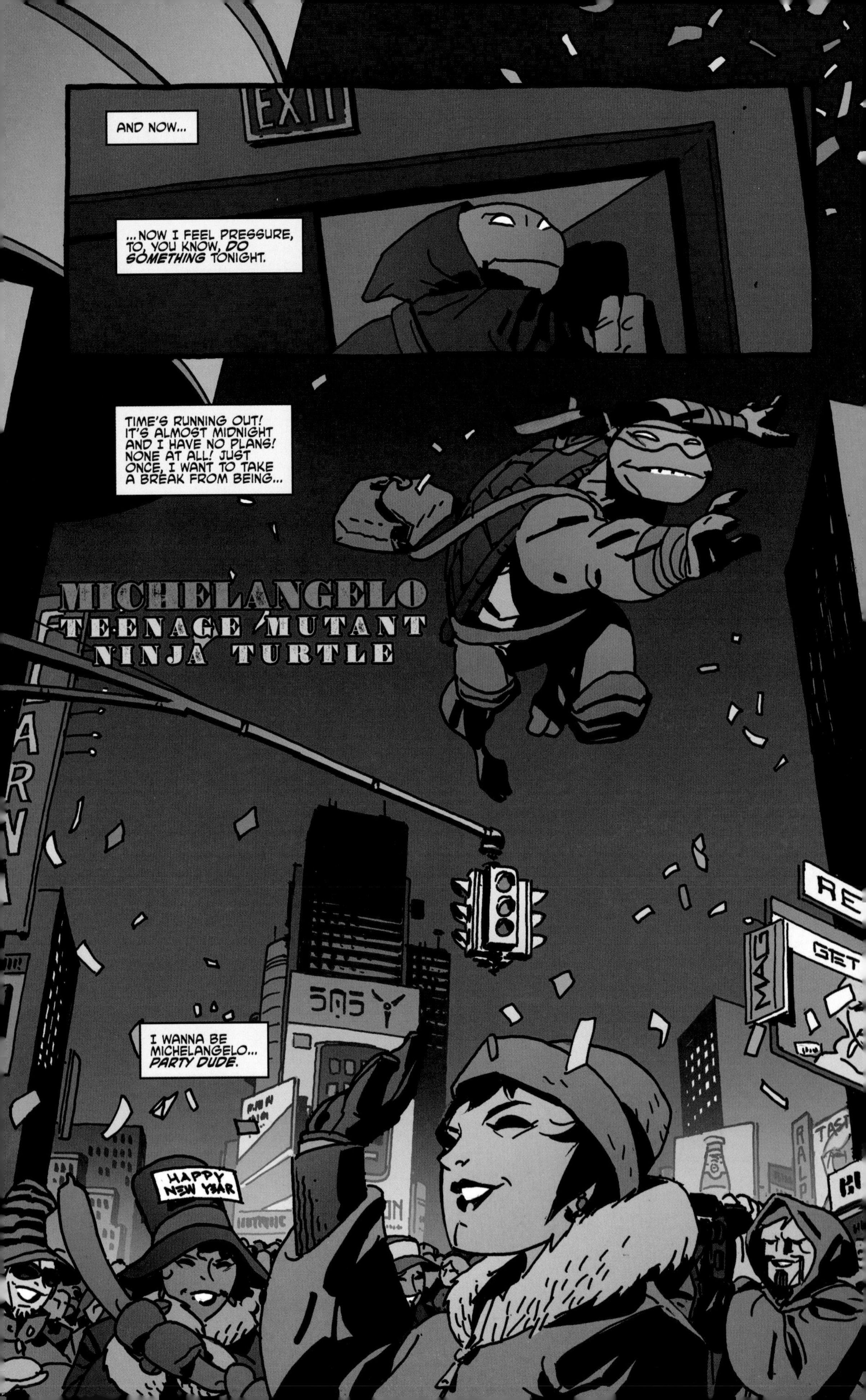
EXIT
AND NOW...
...NOW I FEEL PRESSURE, TO, YOU KNOW, *DO SOMETHING* TONIGHT.
TIME'S RUNNING OUT! IT'S ALMOST MIDNIGHT AND I HAVE NO PLANS! NONE AT ALL! JUST ONCE, I WANT TO TAKE A BREAK FROM BEING...
MICHELANGELO
TEENAGE MUTANT NINJA TURTLE
I WANNA BE MICHELANGELO... *PARTY DUDE*.
HAPPY NEW YEAR

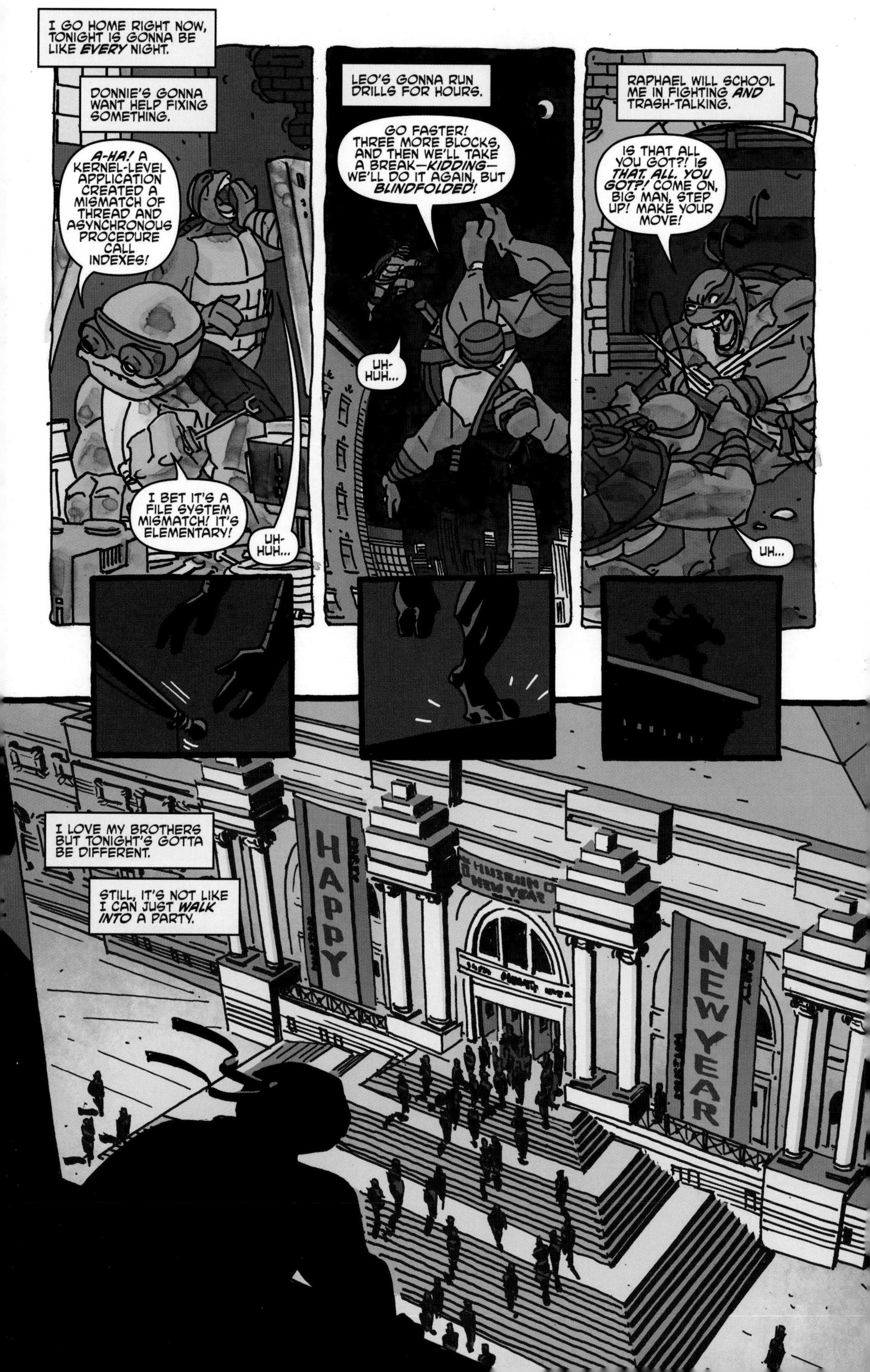
I GO HOME RIGHT NOW, TONIGHT IS GONNA BE LIKE *EVERY* NIGHT.
DONNIE'S GONNA WANT HELP FIXING SOMETHING.
*A-HA!* A KERNEL-LEVEL APPLICATION CREATED A MISMATCH OF THREAD AND ASYNCHRONOUS PROCEDURE CALL INDEXES!
I BET IT'S A FILE SYSTEM MISMATCH! IT'S ELEMENTARY!
UH-HUH...
LEO'S GONNA RUN DRILLS FOR HOURS.
GO FASTER! THREE MORE BLOCKS, AND THEN WE'LL TAKE A BREAK—*KIDDING*—WE'LL DO IT AGAIN, BUT *BLINDFOLDED!*
UH-HUH...
RAPHAEL WILL SCHOOL ME IN FIGHTING *AND* TRASH-TALKING.
IS THAT ALL YOU GOT?! IS *THAT. ALL. YOU GOT?!* COME ON, BIG MAN, STEP UP! MAKE YOUR MOVE!
UH...
I LOVE MY BROTHERS BUT TONIGHT'S GOTTA BE DIFFERENT.
STILL, IT'S NOT LIKE I CAN JUST *WALK INTO* A PARTY.
HAPPY
NEW YEAR

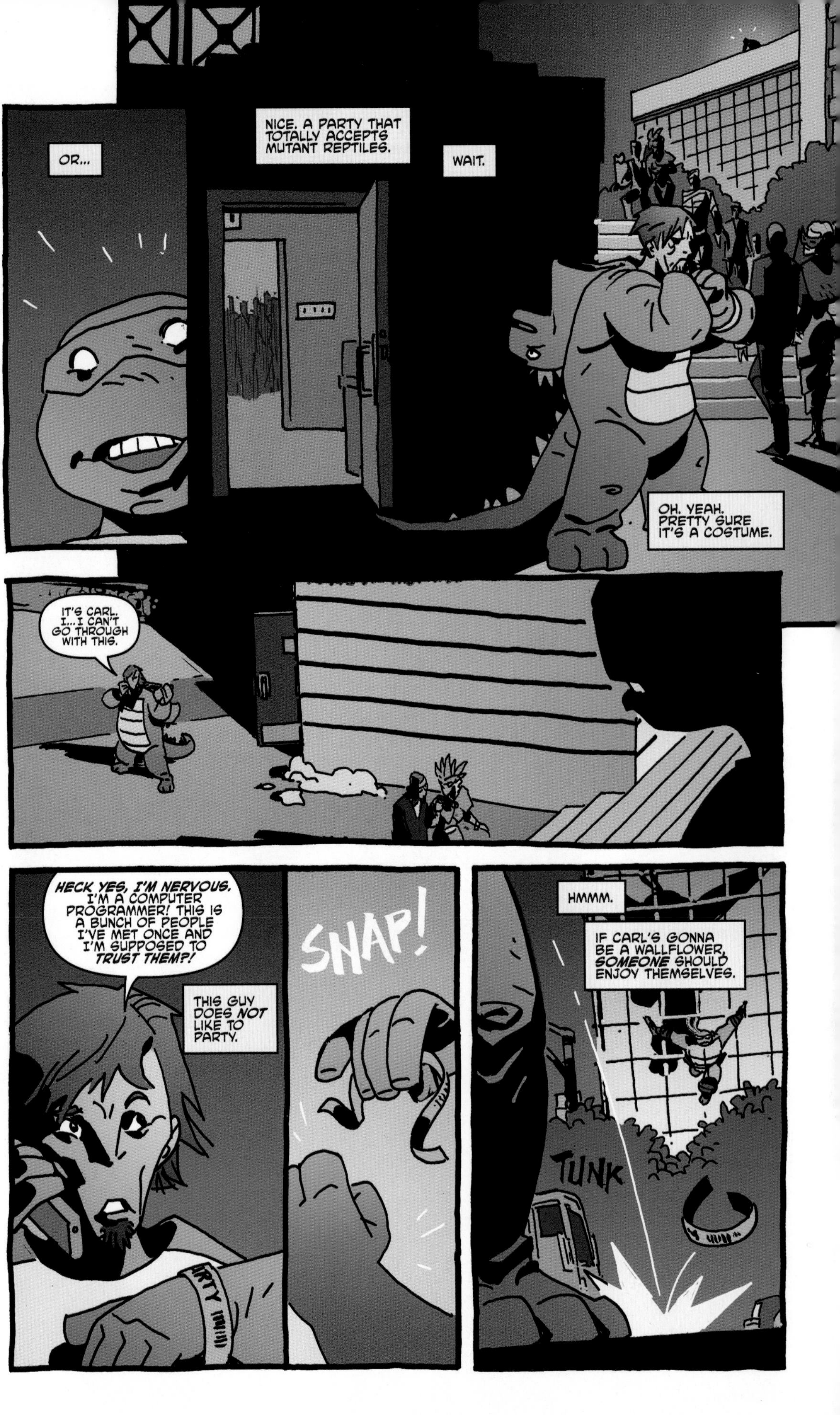

OR...
NICE. A PARTY THAT TOTALLY ACCEPTS MUTANT REPTILES.
WAIT.
OH. YEAH. PRETTY SURE IT'S A COSTUME.
IT'S CARL. I...I CAN'T GO THROUGH WITH THIS.
HECK YES, I'M NERVOUS. I'M A COMPUTER PROGRAMMER! THIS IS A BUNCH OF PEOPLE I'VE MET ONCE AND I'M SUPPOSED TO TRUST THEM?!
THIS GUY DOES NOT LIKE TO PARTY.
SNAP!
HMMM.
IF CARL'S GONNA BE A WALLFLOWER, SOMEONE SHOULD ENJOY THEMSELVES.
TUNK

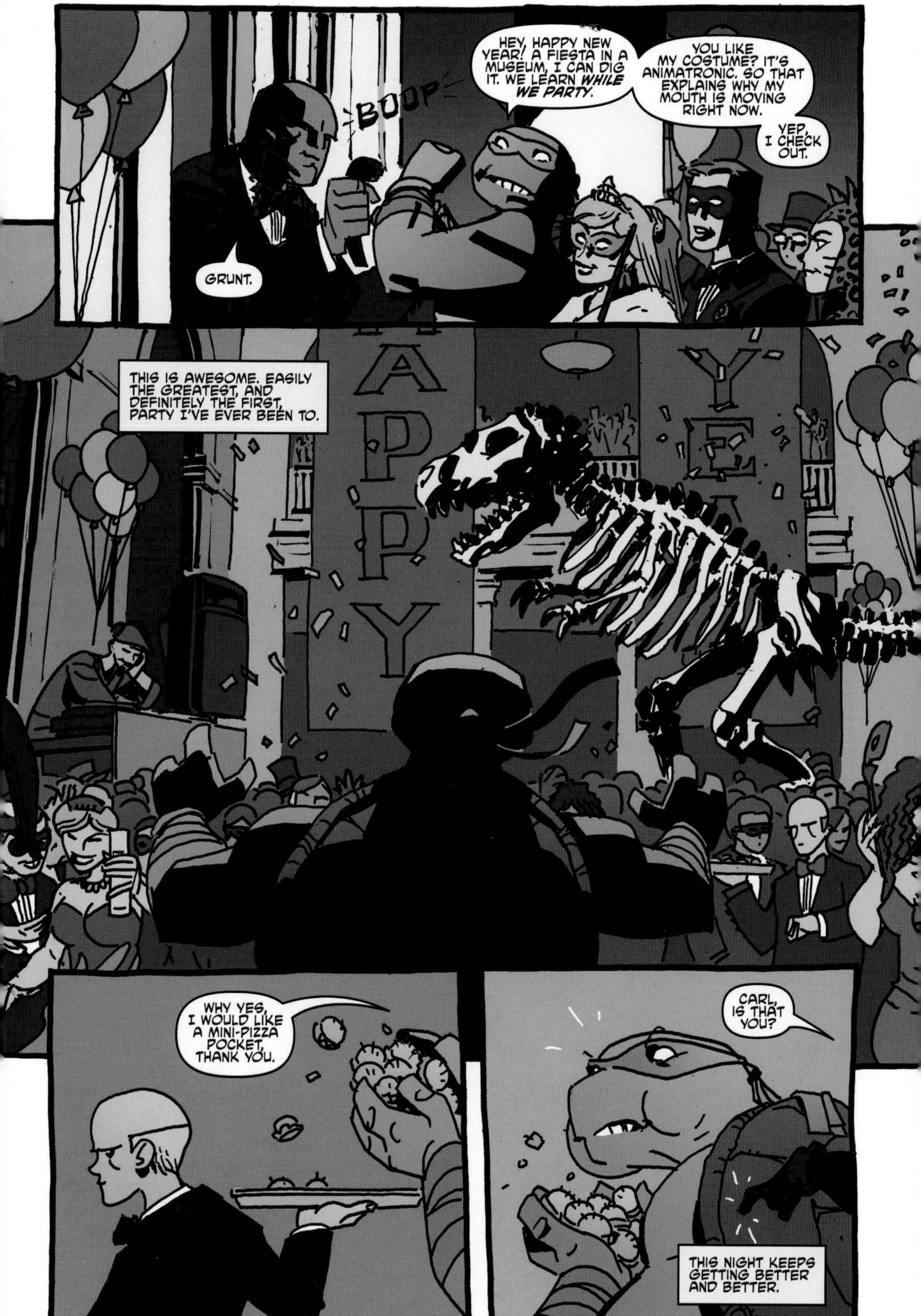
HEY, HAPPY NEW YEAR! A FIESTA IN A MUSEUM, I CAN DIG IT. WE LEARN *WHILE WE PARTY*.
BOOP
YOU LIKE MY COSTUME? IT'S ANIMATRONIC. SO THAT EXPLAINS WHY MY MOUTH IS MOVING RIGHT NOW.
YEP, I CHECK OUT.
GRUNT.
THIS IS AWESOME. EASILY THE GREATEST, AND DEFINITELY THE FIRST, PARTY I'VE EVER BEEN TO.
HAPPY
YE
WHY YES, I WOULD LIKE A MINI-PIZZA POCKET, THANK YOU.
CARL, IS THAT YOU?
THIS NIGHT KEEPS GETTING BETTER AND BETTER.

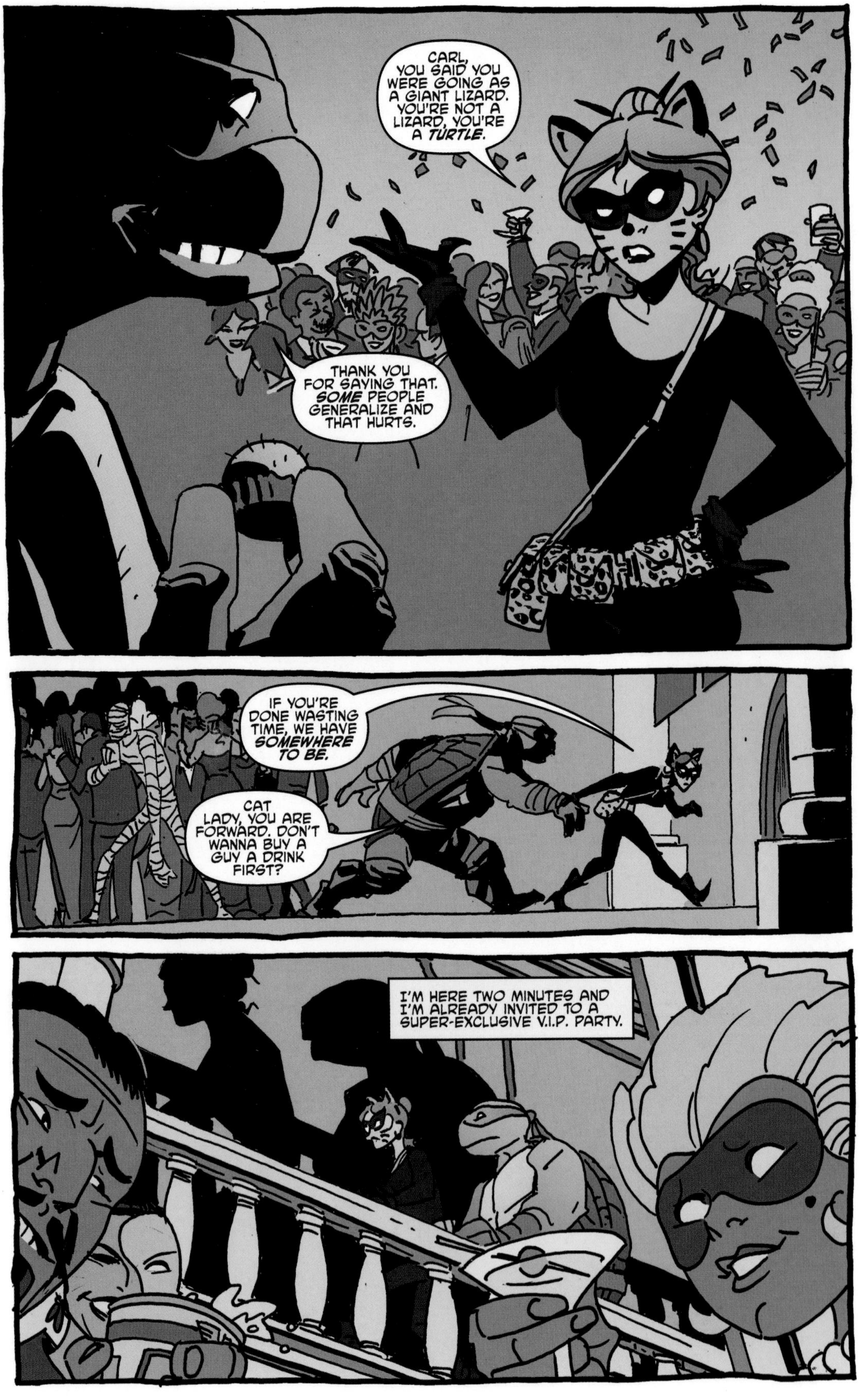
CARL, YOU SAID YOU WERE GOING AS A GIANT LIZARD. YOU'RE NOT A LIZARD, YOU'RE A TURTLE.
THANK YOU FOR SAYING THAT. SOME PEOPLE GENERALIZE AND THAT HURTS.
IF YOU'RE DONE WASTING TIME, WE HAVE SOMEWHERE TO BE.
CAT LADY, YOU ARE FORWARD. DON'T WANNA BUY A GUY A DRINK FIRST?
I'M HERE TWO MINUTES AND I'M ALREADY INVITED TO A SUPER-EXCLUSIVE V.I.P. PARTY.

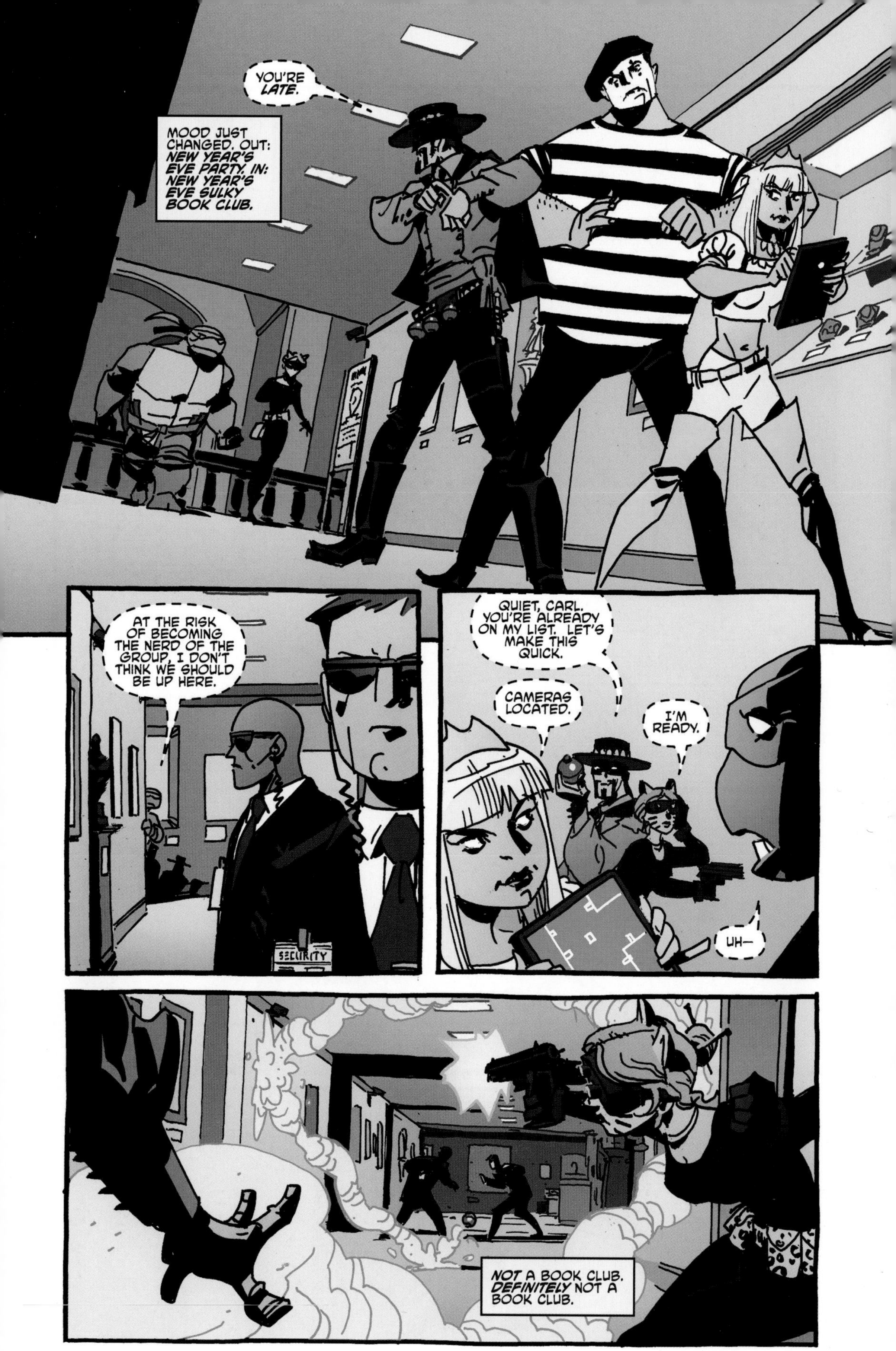
YOU'RE LATE.
MOOD JUST CHANGED. OUT: NEW YEAR'S EVE PARTY. IN: NEW YEAR'S EVE SULKY BOOK CLUB.
AT THE RISK OF BECOMING THE NERD OF THE GROUP, I DON'T THINK WE SHOULD BE UP HERE.
SECURITY
QUIET, CARL. YOU'RE ALREADY ON MY LIST. LET'S MAKE THIS QUICK.
CAMERAS LOCATED.
I'M READY.
UH—
NOT A BOOK CLUB. DEFINITELY NOT A BOOK CLUB.

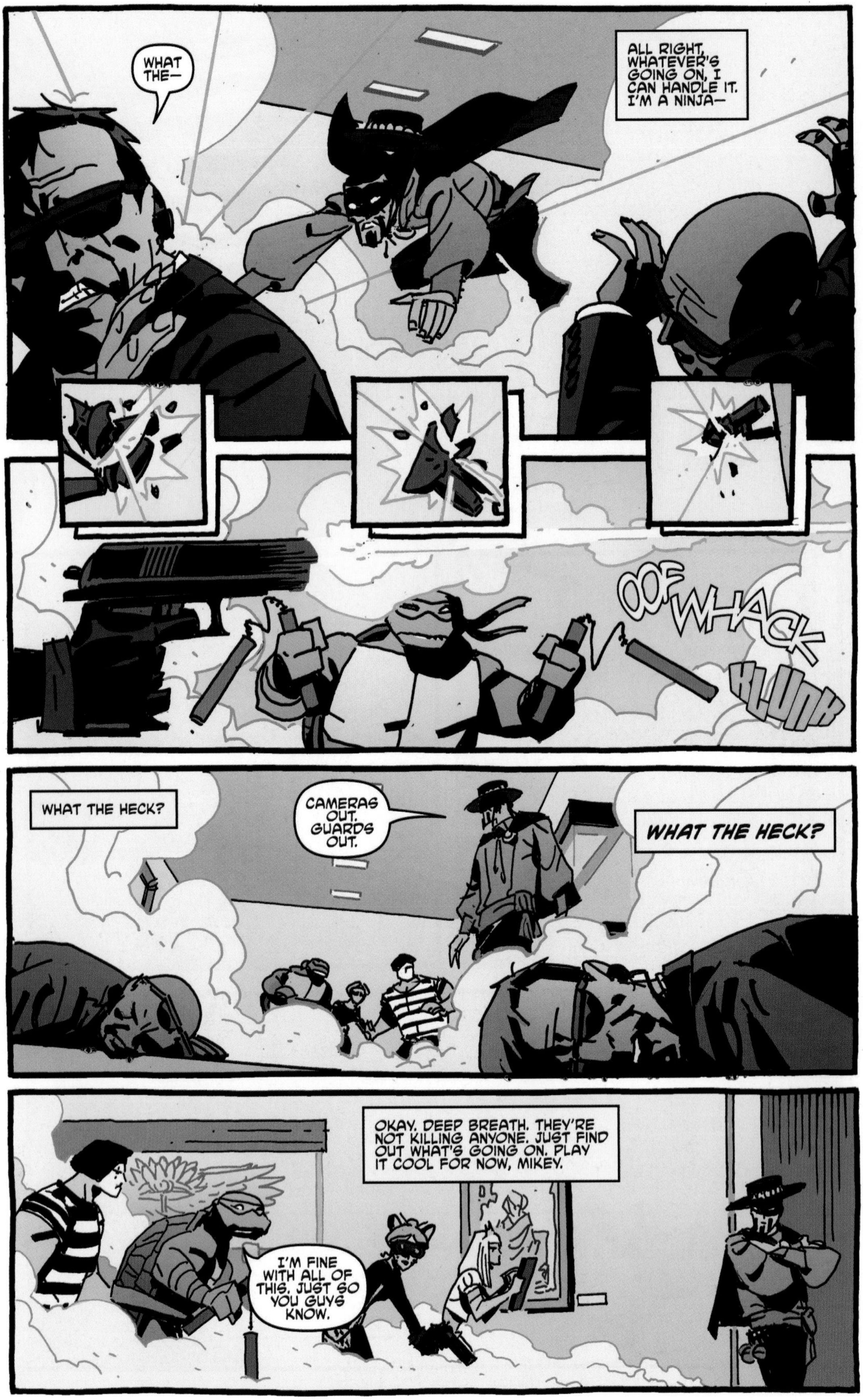
WHAT THE—
ALL RIGHT, WHATEVER'S GOING ON, I CAN HANDLE IT. I'M A NINJA—
OOF
WHACK
KLUNK
WHAT THE HECK?
CAMERAS OUT. GUARDS OUT.
WHAT THE HECK?
OKAY. DEEP BREATH. THEY'RE NOT KILLING ANYONE. JUST FIND OUT WHAT'S GOING ON. PLAY IT COOL FOR NOW, MIKEY.
I'M FINE WITH ALL OF THIS, JUST SO YOU GUYS KNOW.

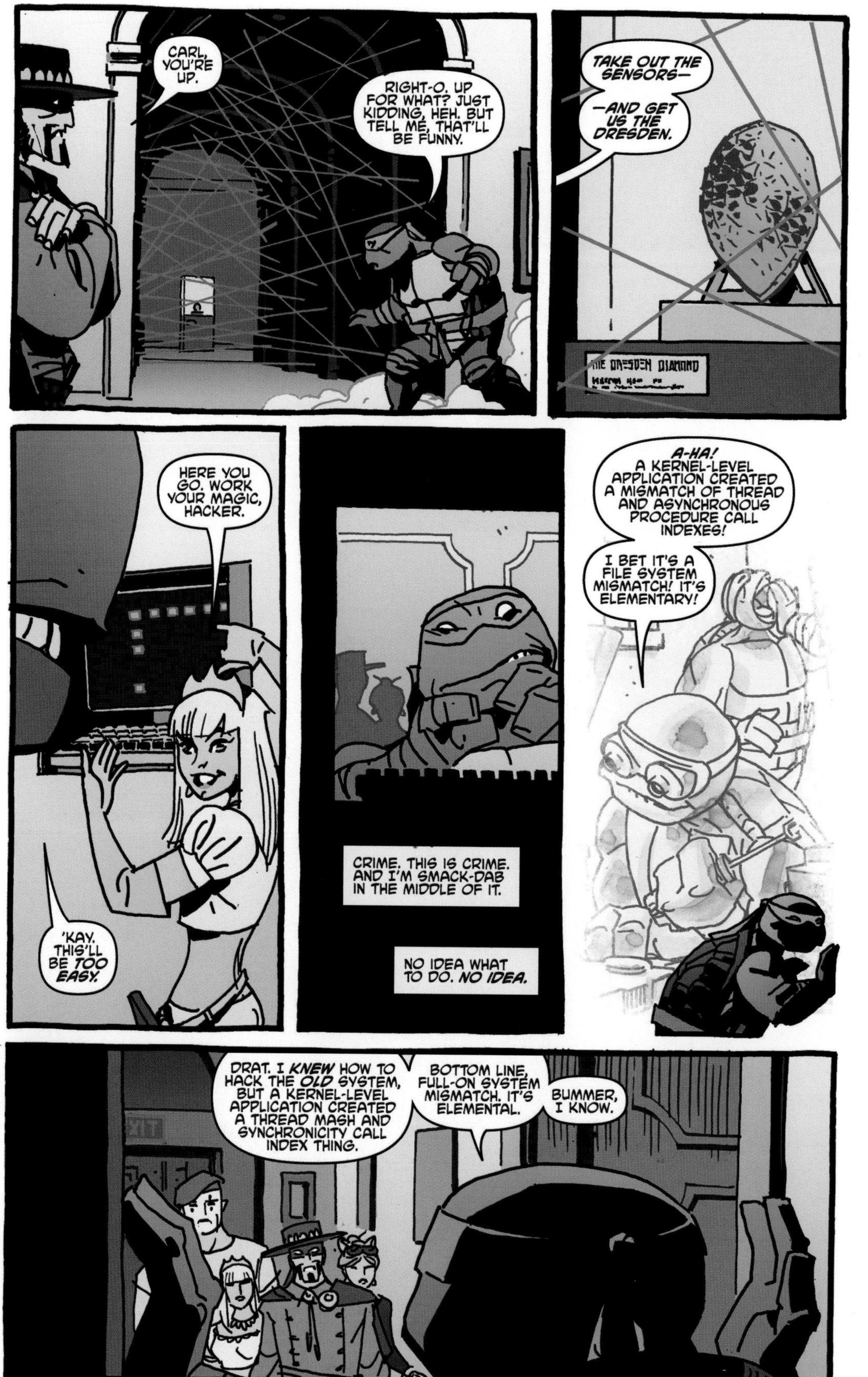

CARL, YOU'RE UP.
RIGHT-O. UP FOR WHAT? JUST KIDDING, HEH. BUT TELL ME, THAT'LL BE FUNNY.
TAKE OUT THE SENSORS—
—AND GET US THE DRESDEN.
THE DRESDEN DIAMOND
HERE YOU GO. WORK YOUR MAGIC, HACKER.
'KAY. THIS'LL BE TOO EASY.
CRIME. THIS IS CRIME. AND I'M SMACK-DAB IN THE MIDDLE OF IT.
NO IDEA WHAT TO DO. NO IDEA.
A-HA! A KERNEL-LEVEL APPLICATION CREATED A MISMATCH OF THREAD AND ASYNCHRONOUS PROCEDURE CALL INDEXES!
I BET IT'S A FILE SYSTEM MISMATCH! IT'S ELEMENTARY!
DRAT. I KNEW HOW TO HACK THE OLD SYSTEM, BUT A KERNEL-LEVEL APPLICATION CREATED A THREAD MASH AND SYNCHRONICITY CALL INDEX THING.
BOTTOM LINE, FULL-ON SYSTEM MISMATCH. IT'S ELEMENTAL.
BUMMER, I KNOW.
EXIT

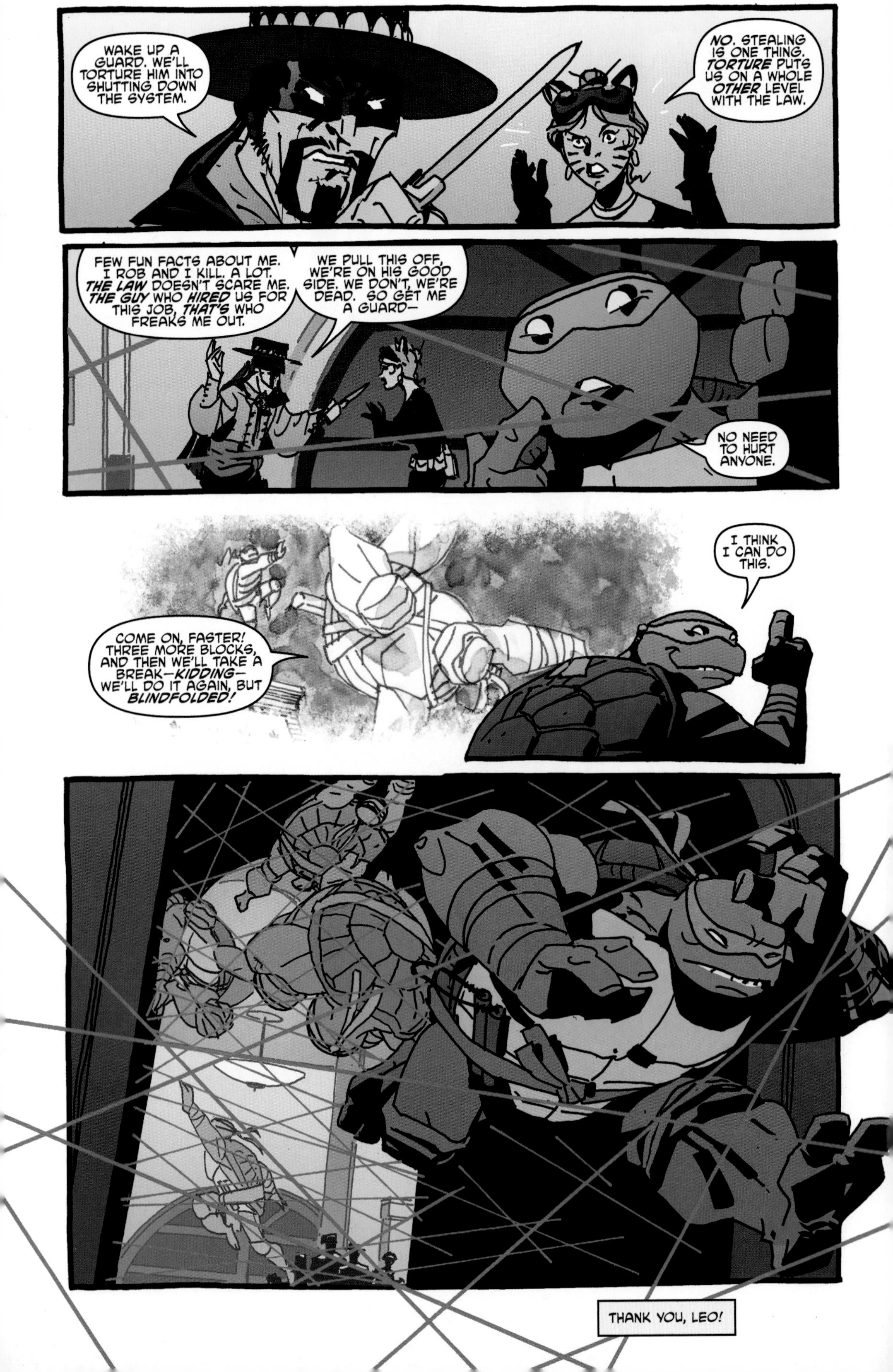
WAKE UP A GUARD. WE'LL TORTURE HIM INTO SHUTTING DOWN THE SYSTEM.
NO. STEALING IS ONE THING. TORTURE PUTS US ON A WHOLE OTHER LEVEL WITH THE LAW.
FEW FUN FACTS ABOUT ME. I ROB AND I KILL. A LOT. THE LAW DOESN'T SCARE ME. THE GUY WHO HIRED US FOR THIS JOB, THAT'S WHO FREAKS ME OUT.
WE PULL THIS OFF, WE'RE ON HIS GOOD SIDE. WE DON'T, WE'RE DEAD. SO GET ME A GUARD—
NO NEED TO HURT ANYONE.
I THINK I CAN DO THIS.
COME ON, FASTER! THREE MORE BLOCKS, AND THEN WE'LL TAKE A BREAK—KIDDING—WE'LL DO IT AGAIN, BUT BLINDFOLDED!
THANK YOU, LEO!

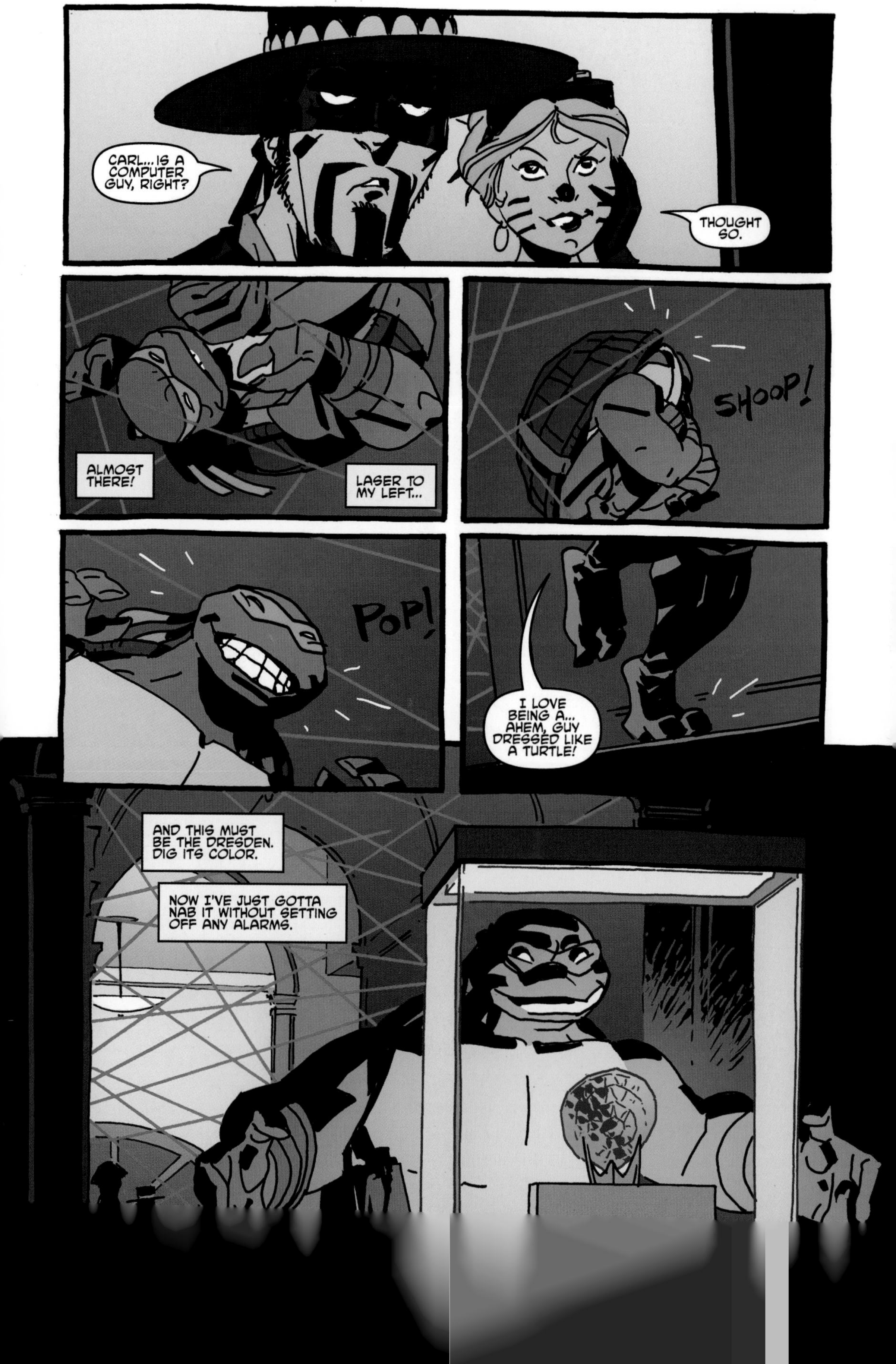
CARL... IS A COMPUTER GUY, RIGHT?
THOUGHT SO.
ALMOST THERE!
LASER TO MY LEFT...
SHOOP!
POP!
I LOVE BEING A... AHEM, GUY DRESSED LIKE A TURTLE!
AND THIS MUST BE THE DRESDEN. DIG ITS COLOR.
NOW I'VE JUST GOTTA NAB IT WITHOUT SETTING OFF ANY ALARMS.

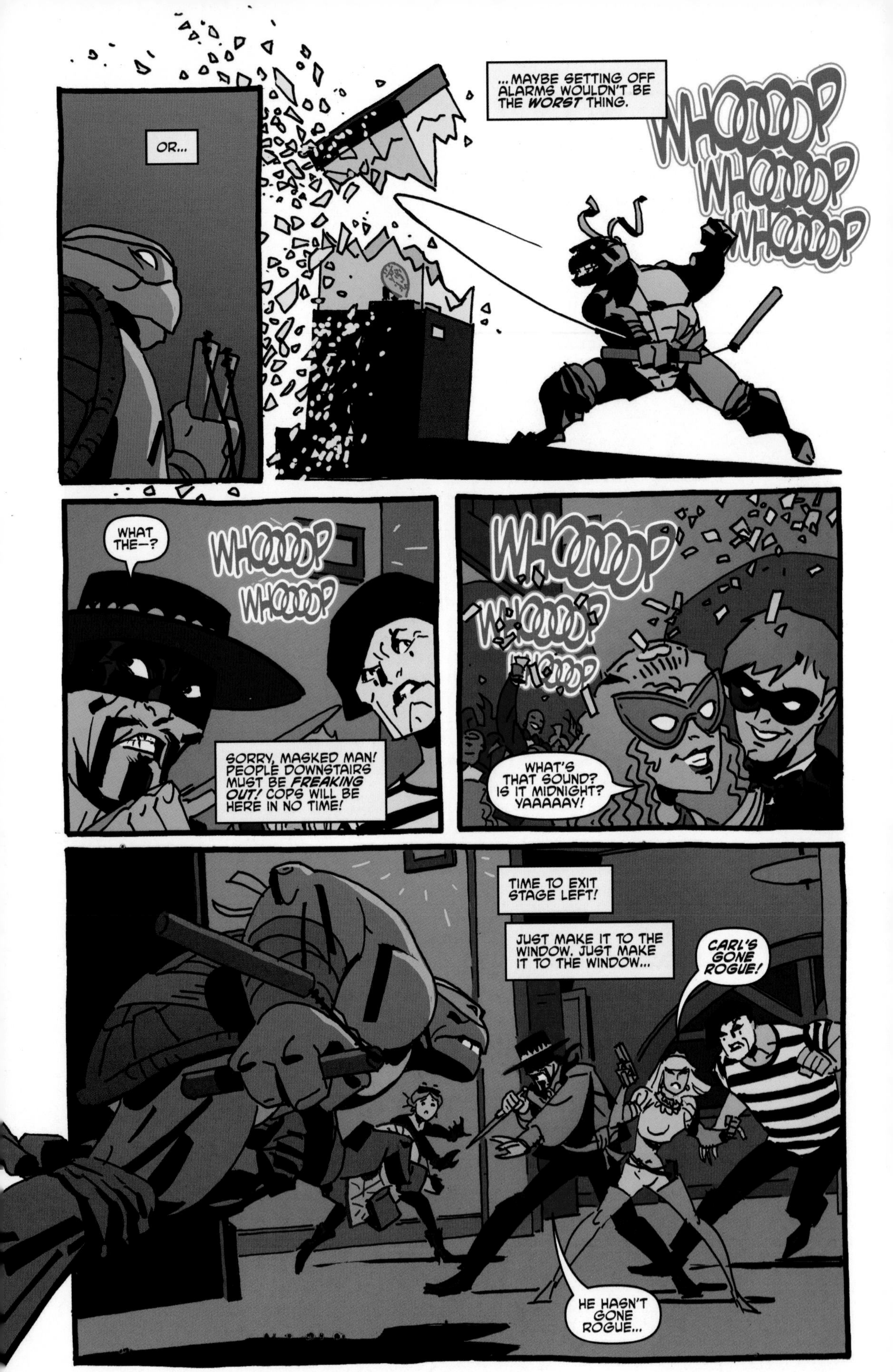
OR...
...MAYBE SETTING OFF ALARMS WOULDN'T BE THE *WORST* THING.
WHOOOOP WHOOOOP WHOOOOP
WHAT THE--?
WHOOOOP WHOOOOP
SORRY, MASKED MAN! PEOPLE DOWNSTAIRS MUST BE *FREAKING OUT!* COPS WILL BE HERE IN NO TIME!
WHOOOOP WHOOOOP WHOOOOP
WHAT'S THAT SOUND? IS IT MIDNIGHT? YAAAAAAY!
TIME TO EXIT STAGE LEFT!
JUST MAKE IT TO THE WINDOW. JUST MAKE IT TO THE WINDOW...
CARL'S GONE ROGUE!
HE HASN'T GONE ROGUE...

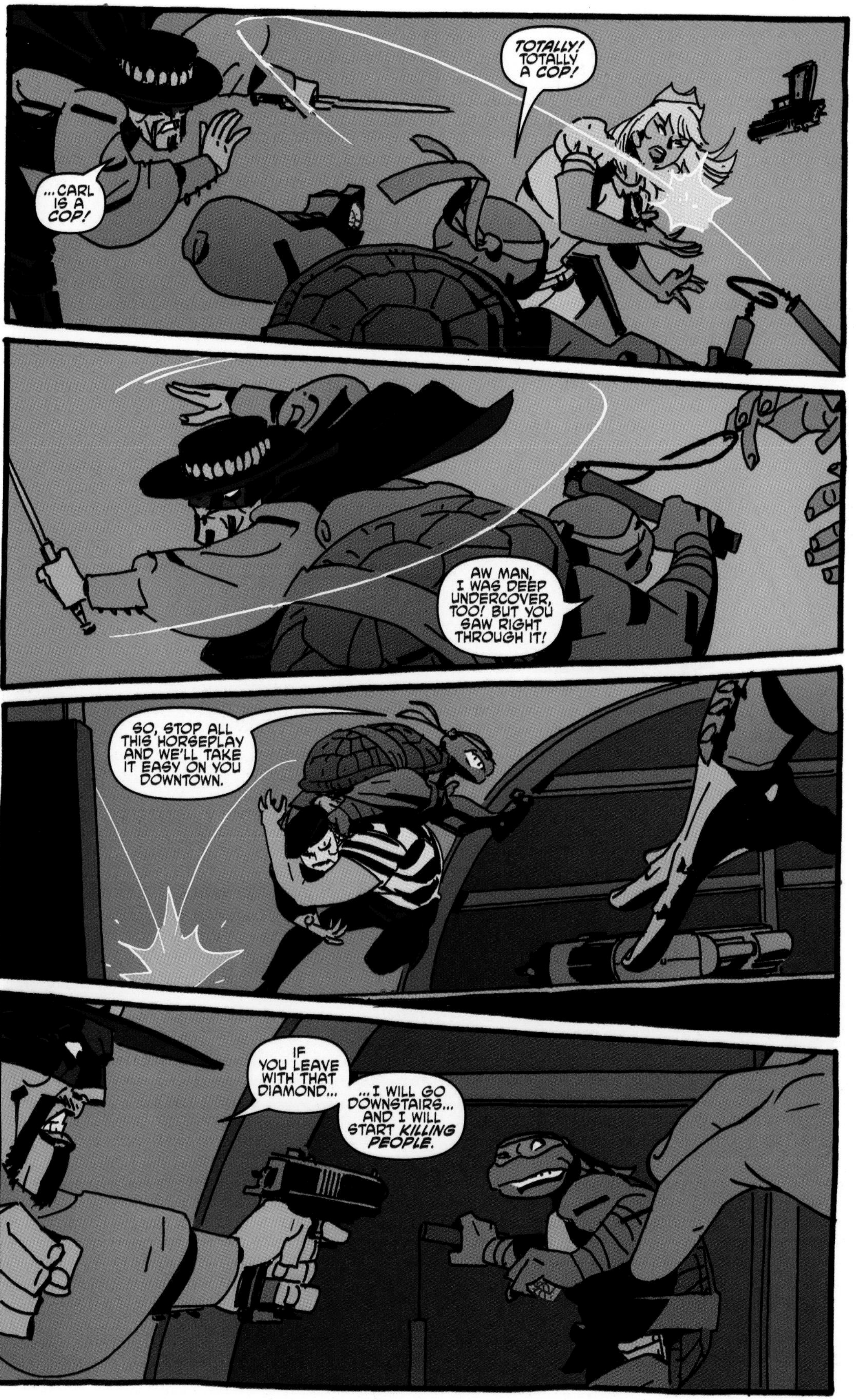
TOTALLY! TOTALLY A COP!
...CARL IS A COP!
AW MAN, I WAS DEEP UNDERCOVER, TOO! BUT YOU SAW RIGHT THROUGH IT!
SO, STOP ALL THIS HORSEPLAY AND WE'LL TAKE IT EASY ON YOU DOWNTOWN.
IF YOU LEAVE WITH THAT DIAMOND...
...I WILL GO DOWNSTAIRS... AND I WILL START KILLING PEOPLE.

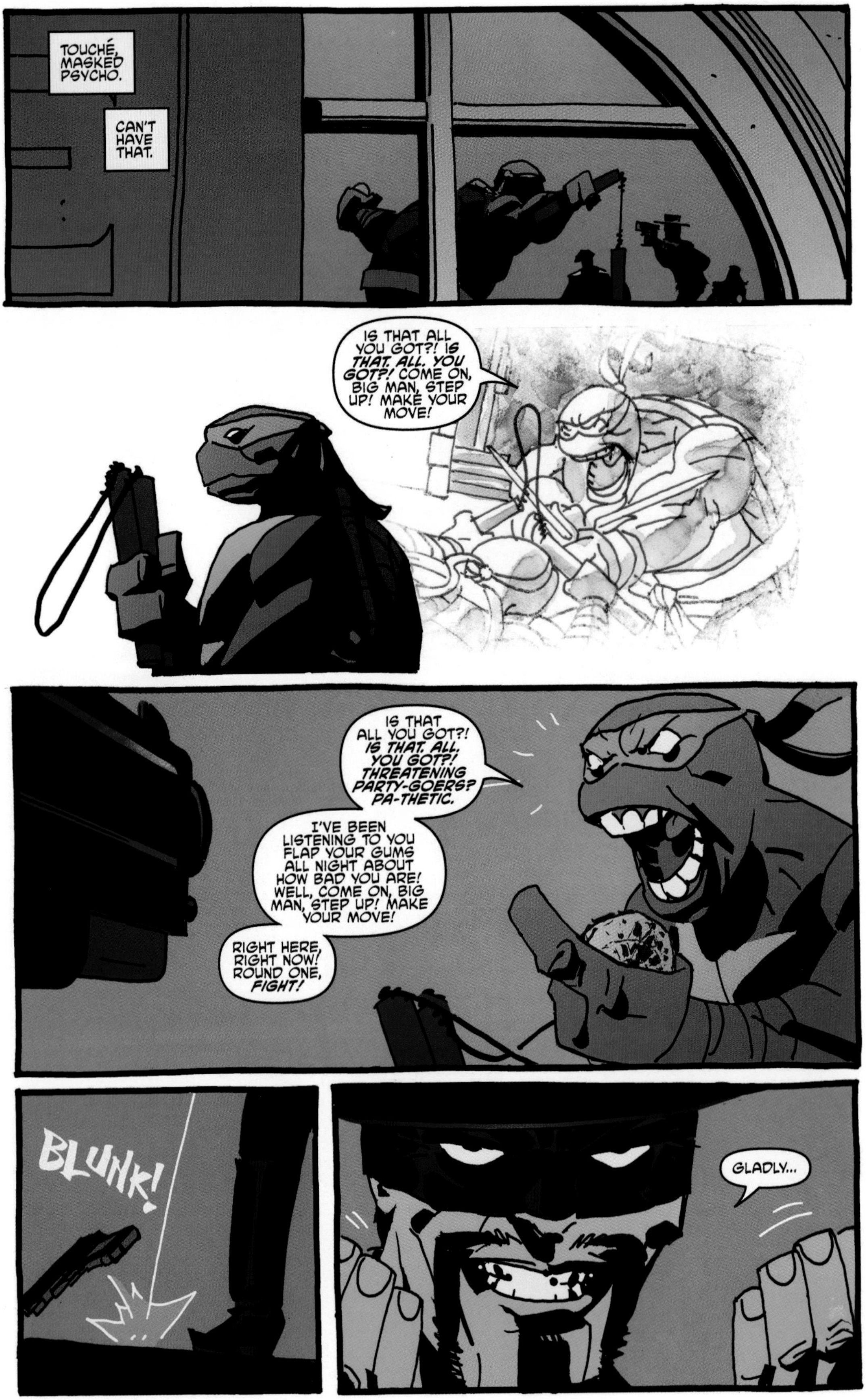

TOUCHÉ, MASKED PSYCHO.
CAN'T HAVE THAT.
IS THAT ALL YOU GOT?! IS *THAT. ALL. YOU GOT?!* COME ON, BIG MAN, STEP UP! MAKE YOUR MOVE!
IS THAT ALL YOU GOT?! *IS THAT. ALL. YOU GOT?! THREATENING PARTY-GOERS? PA-THETIC.*
I'VE BEEN LISTENING TO YOU FLAP YOUR GUMS ALL NIGHT ABOUT HOW BAD YOU ARE! WELL, COME ON, BIG MAN, STEP UP! MAKE YOUR MOVE!
RIGHT HERE, RIGHT NOW! ROUND ONE, *FIGHT!*
BLUNK!
GLADLY...

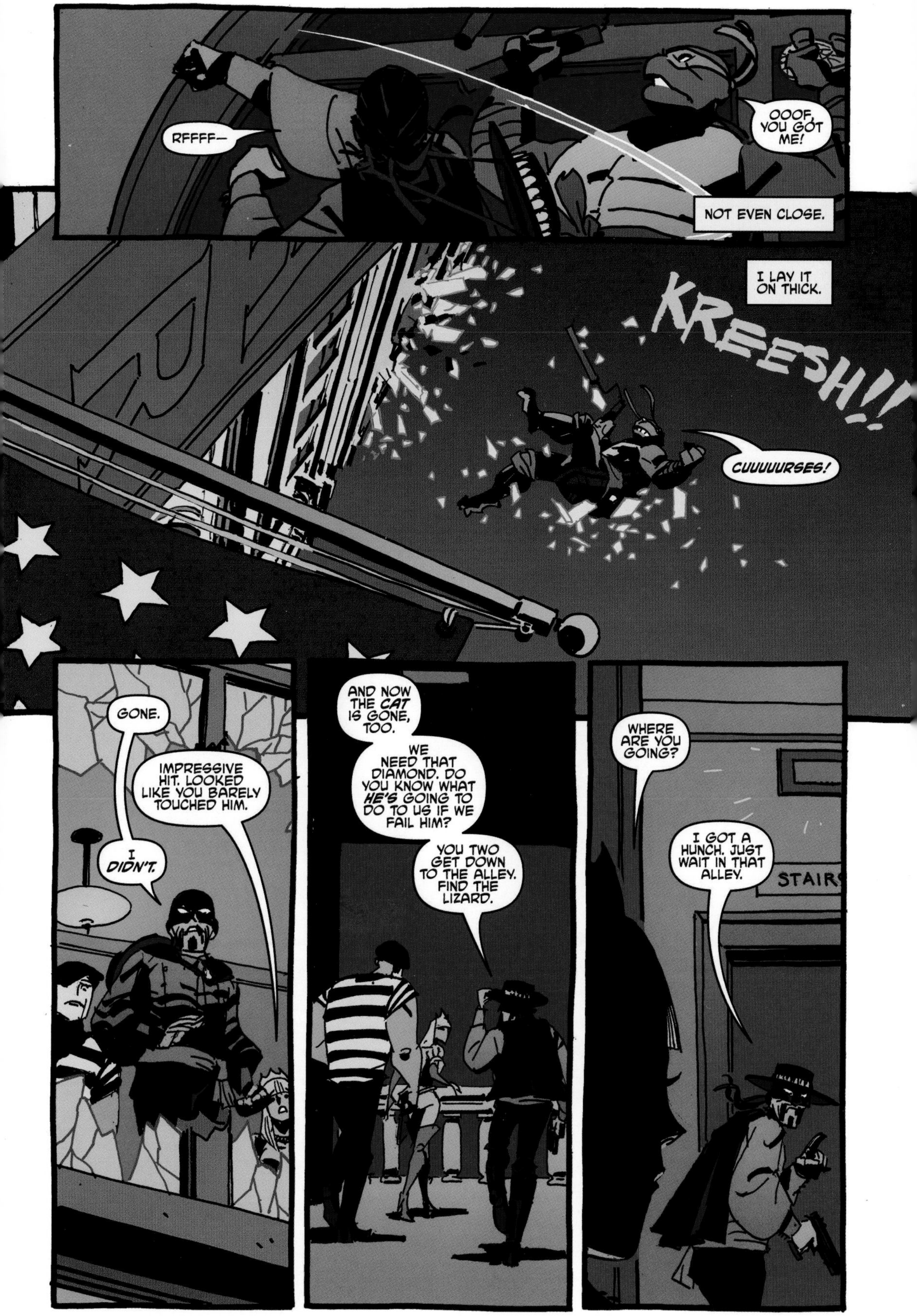
RFFFF—
OOOF, YOU GOT ME!
NOT EVEN CLOSE.
I LAY IT ON THICK.
KREESH!!
CUUUUURSES!
GONE.
IMPRESSIVE HIT. LOOKED LIKE YOU BARELY TOUCHED HIM.
I DIDN'T.
AND NOW THE CAT IS GONE, TOO.
WE NEED THAT DIAMOND. DO YOU KNOW WHAT HE'S GOING TO DO TO US IF WE FAIL HIM?
YOU TWO GET DOWN TO THE ALLEY. FIND THE LIZARD.
WHERE ARE YOU GOING?
I GOT A HUNCH. JUST WAIT IN THAT ALLEY.
STAIRS

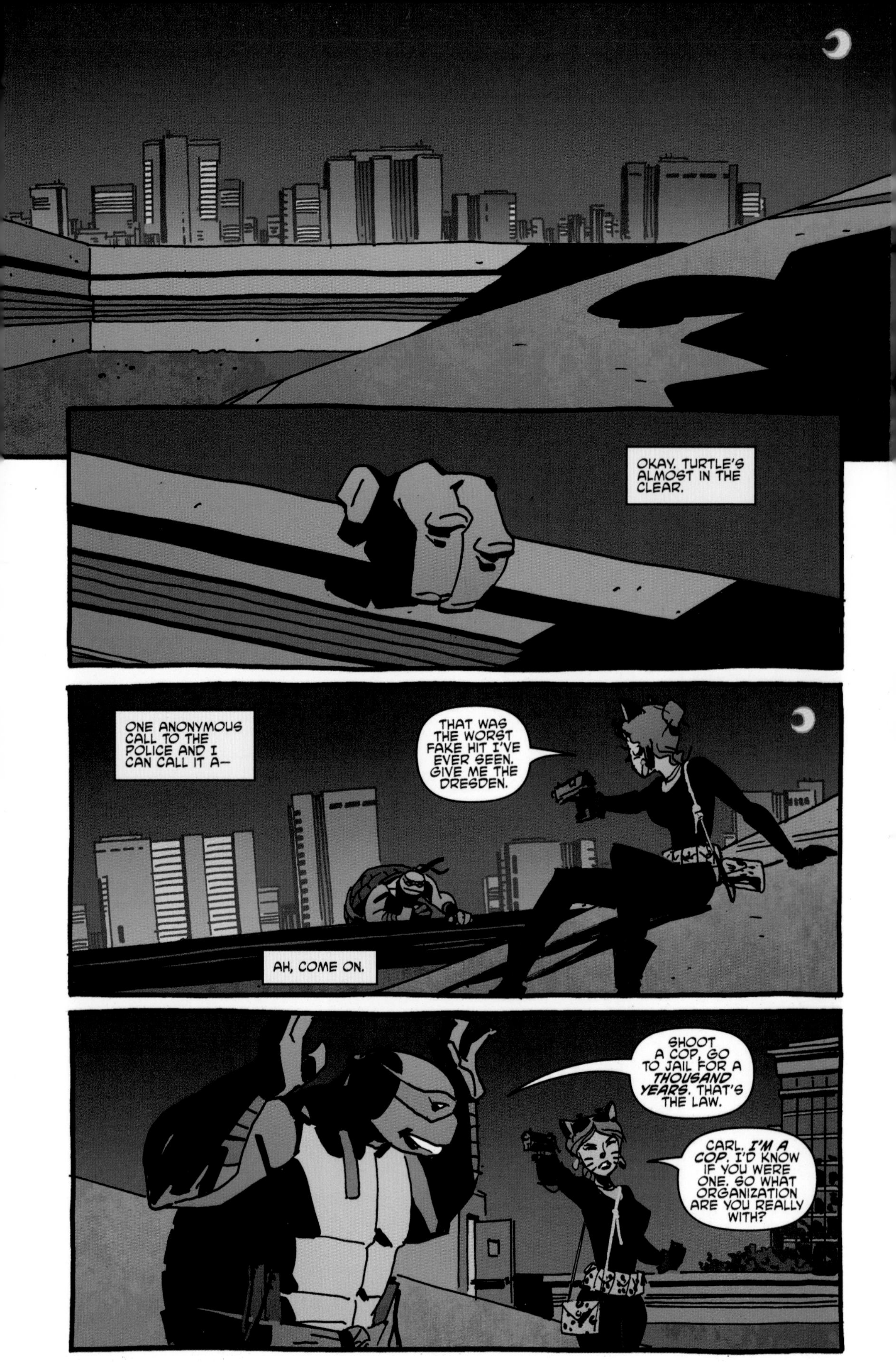
OKAY. TURTLE'S ALMOST IN THE CLEAR.
ONE ANONYMOUS CALL TO THE POLICE AND I CAN CALL IT A—
THAT WAS THE WORST FAKE HIT I'VE EVER SEEN. GIVE ME THE DRESDEN.
AH, COME ON.
SHOOT A COP, GO TO JAIL FOR A THOUSAND YEARS. THAT'S THE LAW.
CARL. I'M A COP. I'D KNOW IF YOU WERE ONE. SO WHAT ORGANIZATION ARE YOU REALLY WITH?

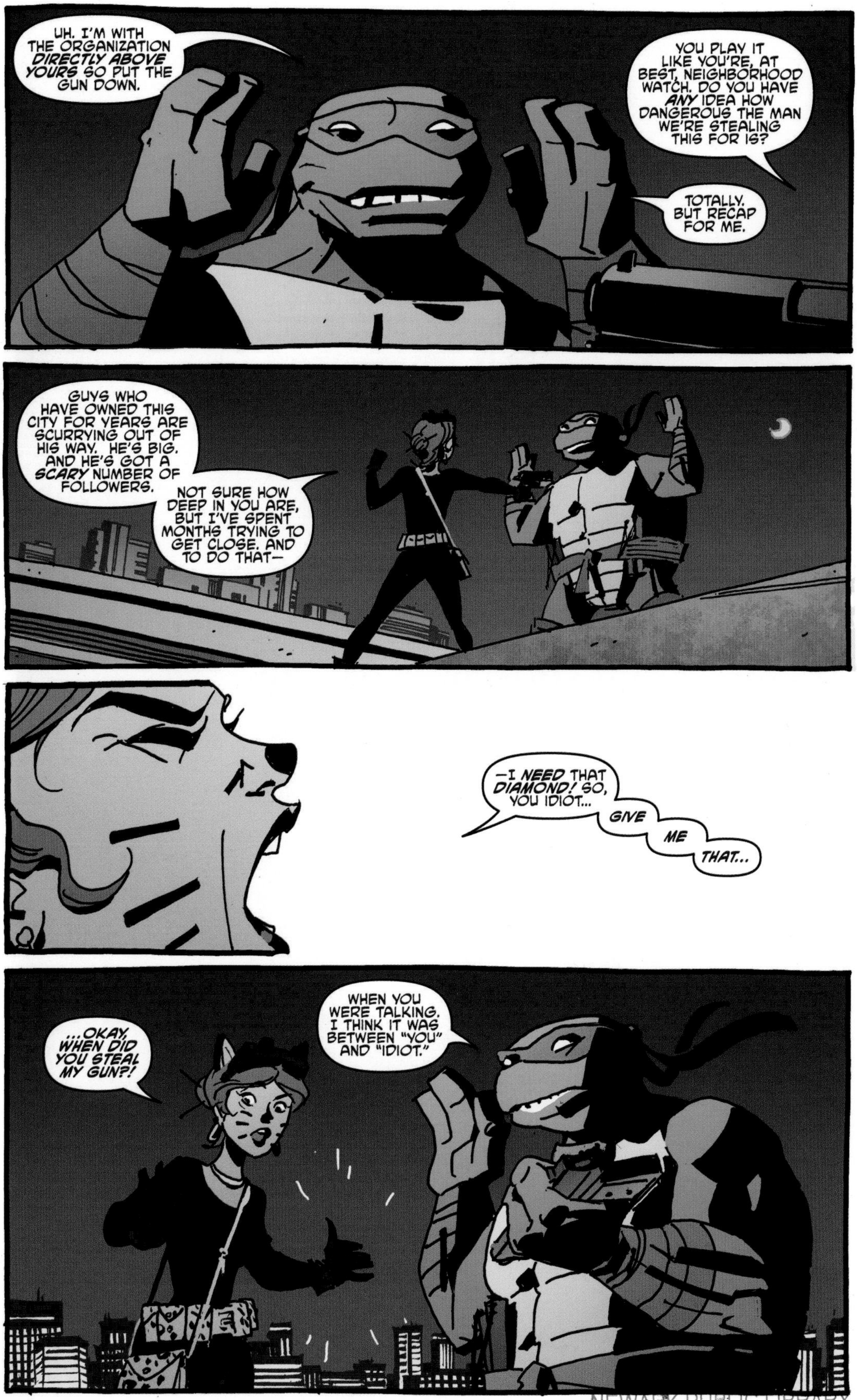
UH. I'M WITH THE ORGANIZATION DIRECTLY ABOVE YOURS SO PUT THE GUN DOWN.
YOU PLAY IT LIKE YOU'RE, AT BEST, NEIGHBORHOOD WATCH. DO YOU HAVE ANY IDEA HOW DANGEROUS THE MAN WE'RE STEALING THIS FOR IS?
TOTALLY. BUT RECAP FOR ME.
GUYS WHO HAVE OWNED THIS CITY FOR YEARS ARE SCURRYING OUT OF HIS WAY. HE'S BIG. AND HE'S GOT A SCARY NUMBER OF FOLLOWERS.
NOT SURE HOW DEEP IN YOU ARE, BUT I'VE SPENT MONTHS TRYING TO GET CLOSE. AND TO DO THAT—
—I NEED THAT DIAMOND! SO, YOU IDIOT...
GIVE
ME
THAT...
...OKAY, WHEN DID YOU STEAL MY GUN?!
WHEN YOU WERE TALKING. I THINK IT WAS BETWEEN "YOU" AND "IDIOT."

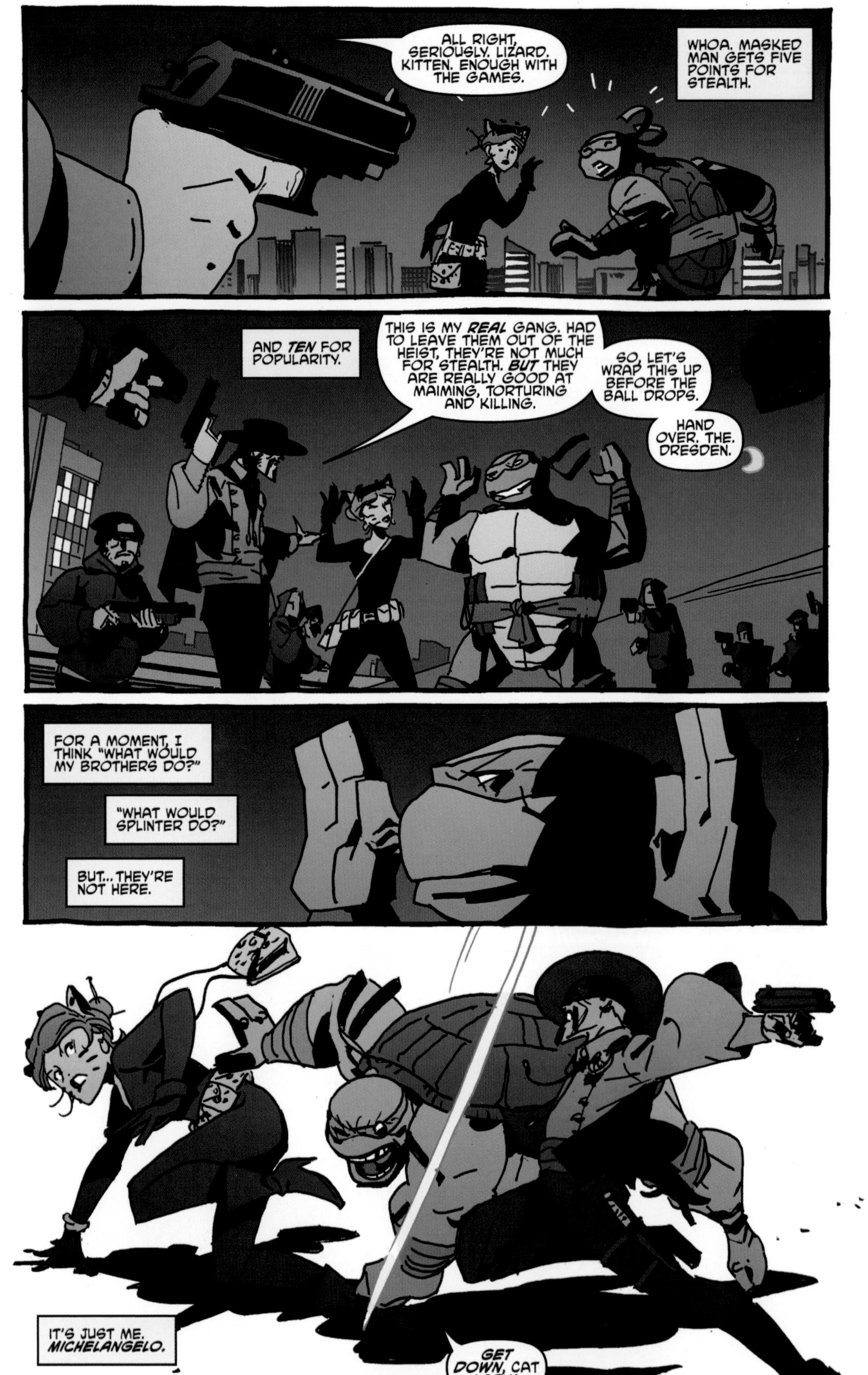
ALL RIGHT, SERIOUSLY. LIZARD. KITTEN. ENOUGH WITH THE GAMES.
WHOA. MASKED MAN GETS FIVE POINTS FOR STEALTH.
AND *TEN* FOR POPULARITY.
THIS IS MY *REAL* GANG. HAD TO LEAVE THEM OUT OF THE HEIST, THEY'RE NOT MUCH FOR STEALTH. *BUT* THEY ARE REALLY GOOD AT MAIMING, TORTURING AND KILLING.
SO, LET'S WRAP THIS UP BEFORE THE BALL DROPS.
HAND OVER. THE. DRESDEN.
FOR A MOMENT, I THINK "WHAT WOULD MY BROTHERS DO?"
"WHAT WOULD SPLINTER DO?"
BUT... THEY'RE NOT HERE.
IT'S JUST ME. *MICHELANGELO.*
*GET DOWN,* CAT LADY!

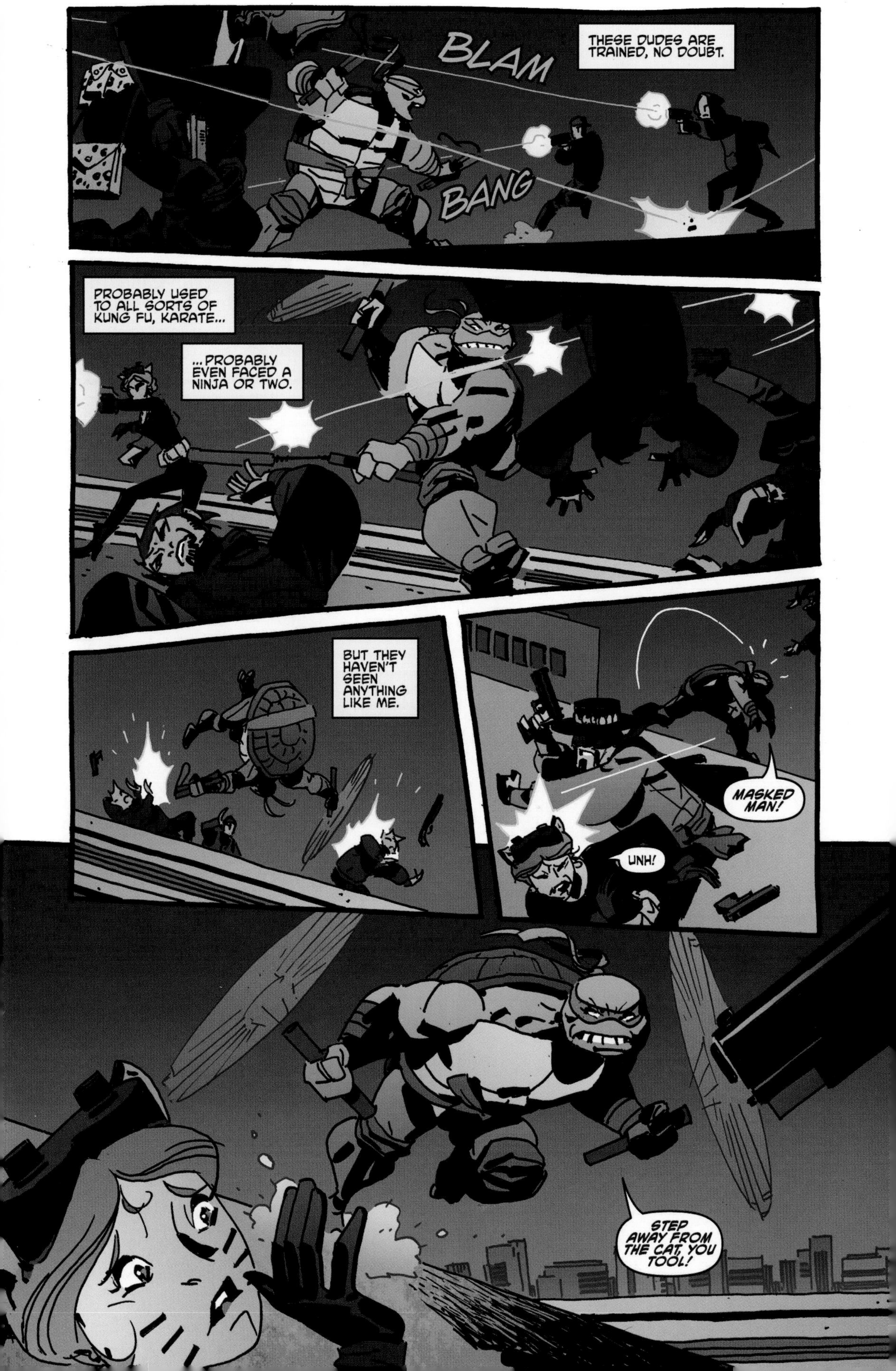
BLAM
THESE DUDES ARE TRAINED, NO DOUBT.
BANG
PROBABLY USED TO ALL SORTS OF KUNG FU, KARATE...
...PROBABLY EVEN FACED A NINJA OR TWO.
BUT THEY HAVEN'T SEEN ANYTHING LIKE ME.
MASKED MAN!
UNH!
STEP AWAY FROM THE CAT, YOU TOOL!

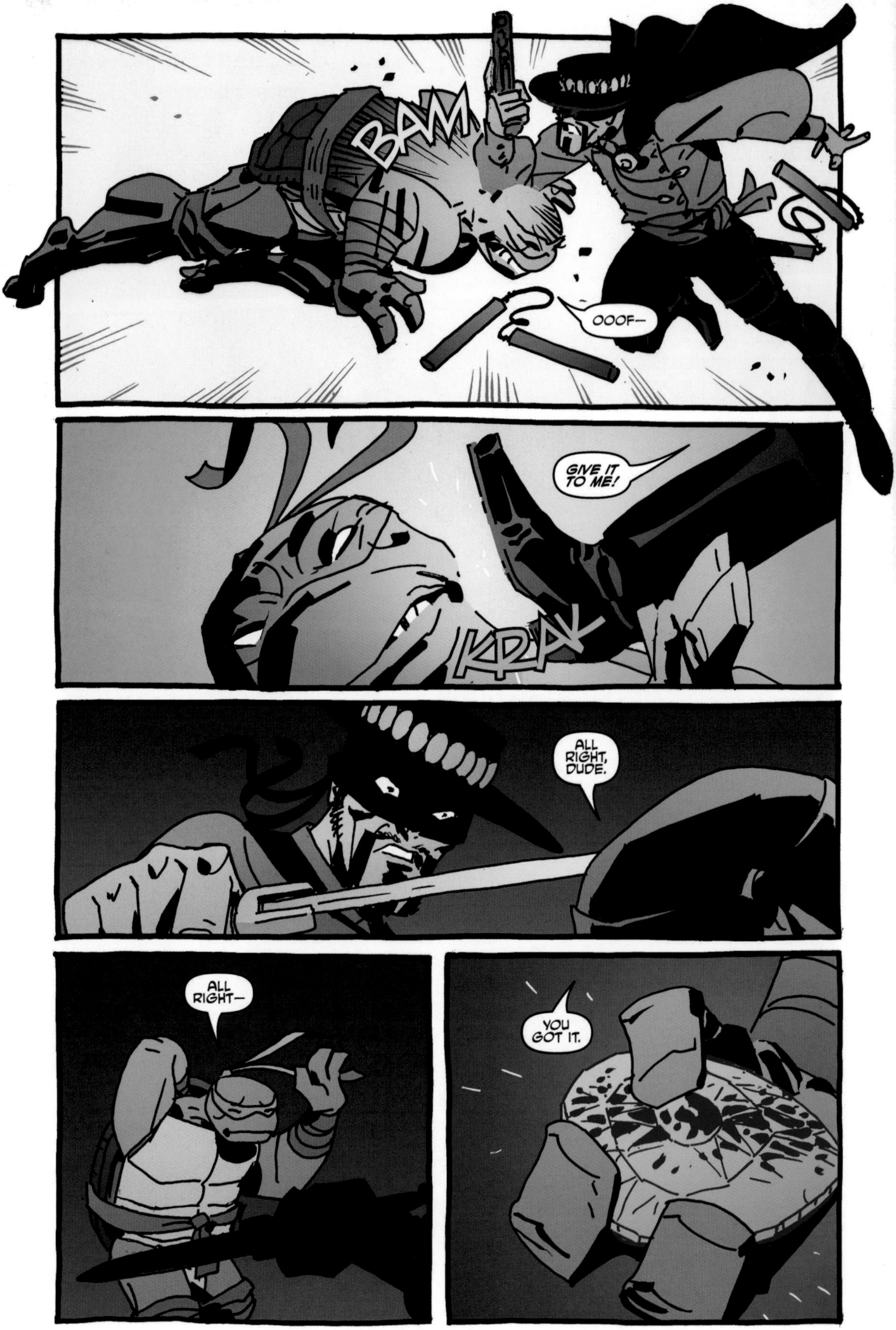
BAM
OOOF—
GIVE IT TO ME!
KRAK
ALL RIGHT, DUDE.
ALL RIGHT—
YOU GOT IT.

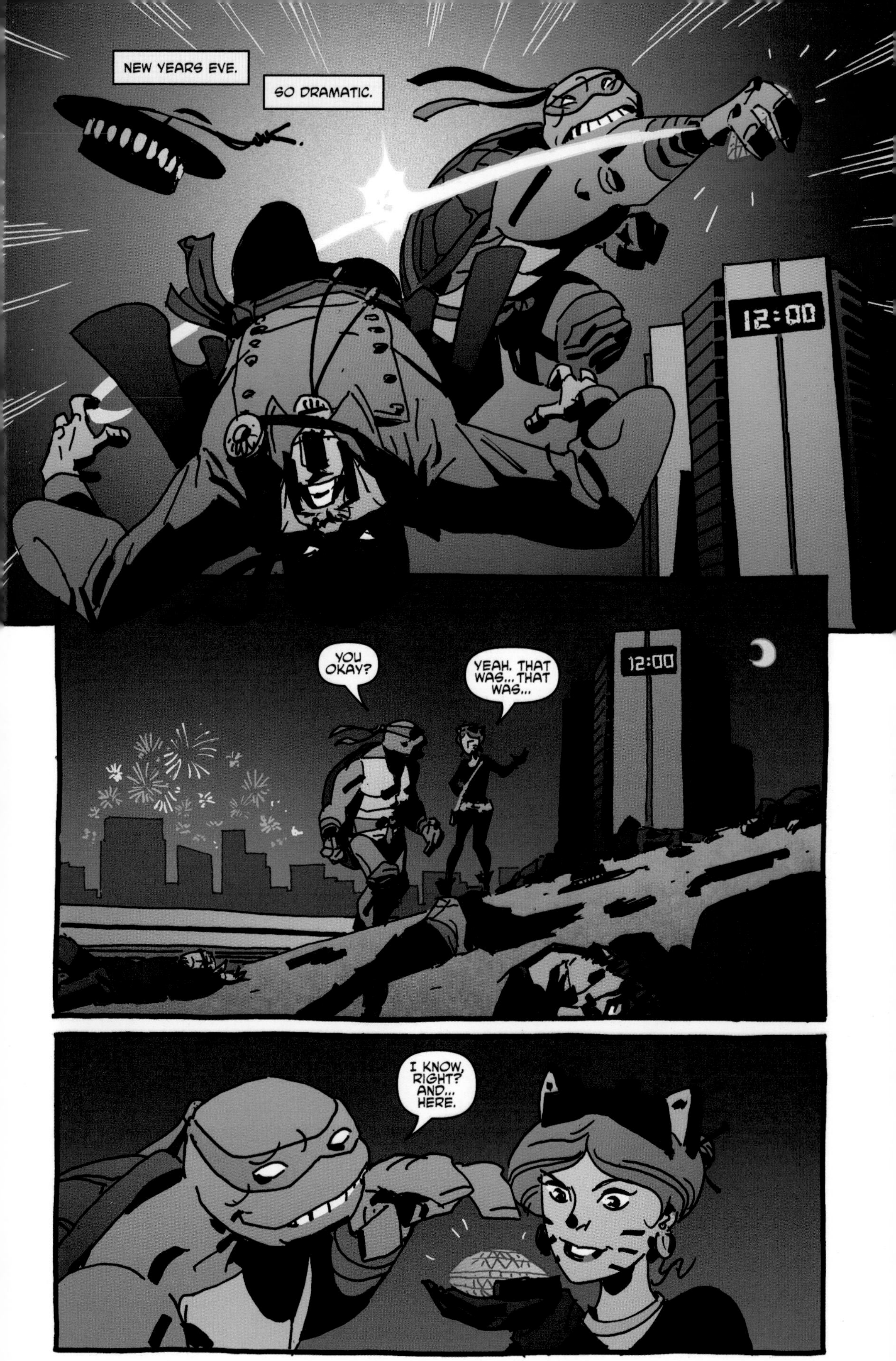
NEW YEARS EVE.
SO DRAMATIC.
12:00
12:00
YOU OKAY?
YEAH. THAT WAS... THAT WAS...
I KNOW, RIGHT? AND... HERE.

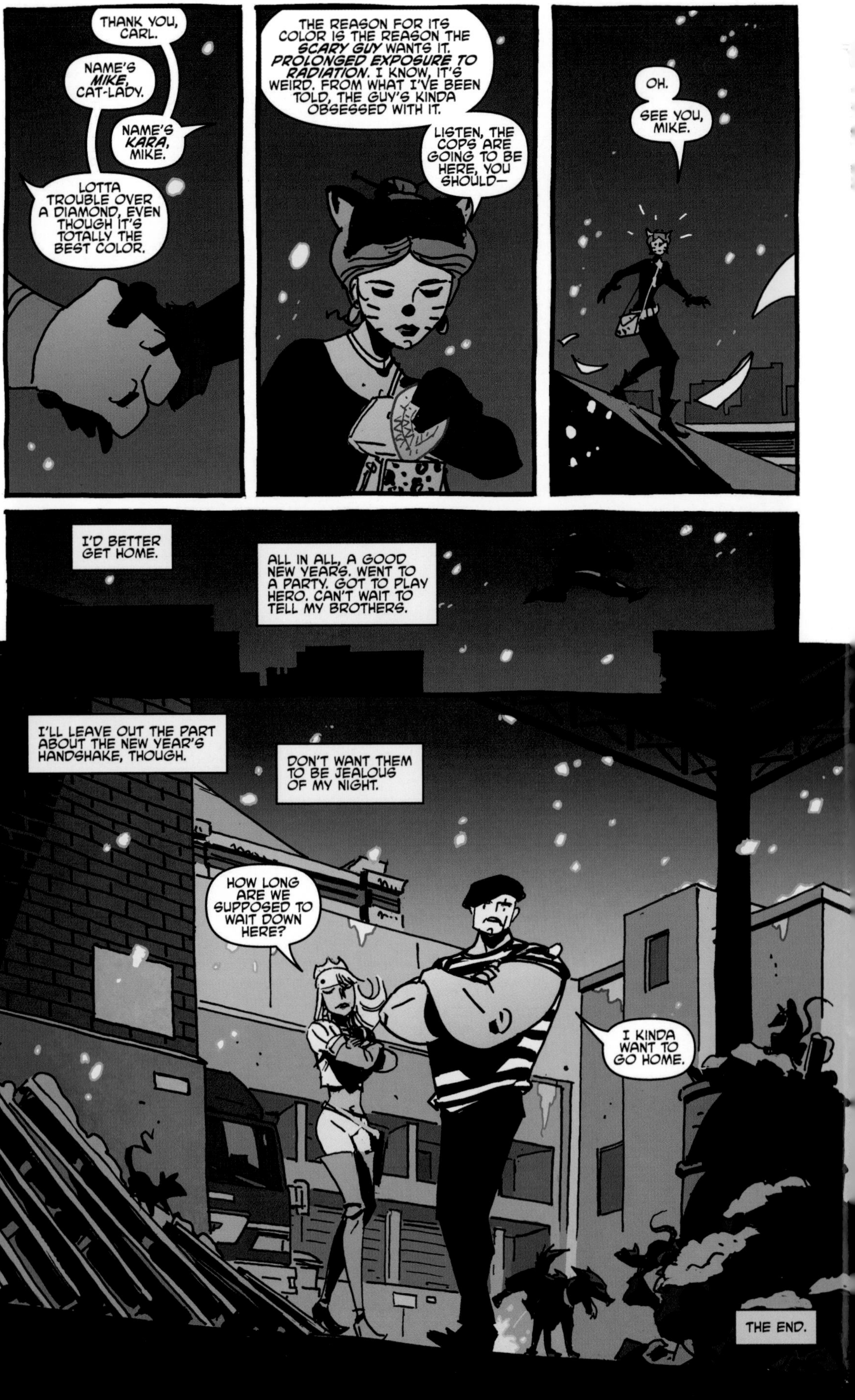
THANK YOU, CARL.
NAME'S MIKE, CAT-LADY.
NAME'S KARA, MIKE.
LOTTA TROUBLE OVER A DIAMOND, EVEN THOUGH IT'S TOTALLY THE BEST COLOR.
THE REASON FOR ITS COLOR IS THE REASON THE SCARY GUY WANTS IT. PROLONGED EXPOSURE TO RADIATION. I KNOW, IT'S WEIRD. FROM WHAT I'VE BEEN TOLD, THE GUY'S KINDA OBSESSED WITH IT.
LISTEN, THE COPS ARE GOING TO BE HERE, YOU SHOULD—
OH.
SEE YOU, MIKE.
I'D BETTER GET HOME.
ALL IN ALL, A GOOD NEW YEARS. WENT TO A PARTY. GOT TO PLAY HERO. CAN'T WAIT TO TELL MY BROTHERS.
I'LL LEAVE OUT THE PART ABOUT THE NEW YEAR'S HANDSHAKE, THOUGH.
DON'T WANT THEM TO BE JEALOUS OF MY NIGHT.
HOW LONG ARE WE SUPPOSED TO WAIT DOWN HERE?
I KINDA WANT TO GO HOME.
THE END.